BITES

BIGGER BITES FOR BIGGER READERS!

CRAZY for CAKE

Rick Bickworth has decided
he is average. Not good, not bad,
just average. Then Rick
makes a discovery—he is born to bake!
The problem is, Rick is now
in competition with his mom.

How can he keep baking
and keep the peace?

MORE BITES TO SINK YOUR TEETH INTO!

THE GUTLESS GLADIATOR
Margaret Clark
Illustrated by Terry Denton

LET IT RIP!
Archimede Fusillo
Illustrated by Stephen Michael King

LUKE AND LULU
Bruce Davis
Illustrated by Chantal Stewart

MISS WOLF AND THE PORKERS
Bill Condon
Illustrated by Caroline Magerl

THE TOO-TIGHT TUTU
Sherryl Clark
Illustrated by Cathy Wilcox

CAN RICK BAKE THE BEST CAKE?

Phillip Gwynne
Illustrated by Gus Gordon

RUNNING PRESS
KIDS
PHILADELPHIA·LONDON

To the Goldbug, thanks for the idea—P.G.

For Ollie, who loves cake—G.G.

First published by Penguin Group (Australia),
a division of Pearson Australia Group Pty Ltd, 2005

First published in the United States
by Running Press Book Publishers, 2007

Printed in China

9   8   7   6   5   4   3   2   1
Digit on the right indicates the number of this printing

Library of Congress Control Number: 2006929398
ISBN-13: 978-0-7624-2923-3
ISBN-10: 0-7624-2923-2

Original design by Karen Trump and Ruth Grüner,
Penguin Group (Australia).
Additional design for this edition by Frances J. Soo Ping Chow

Typography: New Century School Book
This book may be ordered by mail from the publisher.
Please include $2.50 for postage and handling.
But try your bookstore first!

This edition published by Running Press Kids, an imprint of
Running Press Book Publishers
2300 Chestnut Street
Philadelphia, PA 19103-4371

Visit us on the web!
www.runningpress.com

Ages 7–10
Grades 2–4

1

AVERAGE

"Average," said Mr. McPhee. "Who can tell me what that means?"

Sally Quickfire's arm went up first. Sally Quickfire's arm always went up first. It was spring-loaded: the fastest arm in sixth grade of Cobdolla Elementary School.

"Yes, Sally," said Mr. McPhee.

Sally looked around triumphantly before she answered. "It means in the middle. Neither good nor bad."

"That's right, Sally," said Mr. McPhee. "Not good. Not bad. Middle-of-the-road."

Rick Bickworth, sitting in the back row, was sure Mr. McPhee was looking right at him when he said this. His eyes were boring into his. He's really got it in for me, thought Rick. Just because I'm the second biggest boy in the school and I don't play on his stupid football team. And then he remembered what they said on the playground—McPhee, McPhee, brain the size of a pea—and he smiled.

"Rick Bickworth! What's so funny?" said Mr. McPhee.

"Nothing, Mr. Pea . . . I mean
McPhee."

"Then perhaps you'd like to remind
the class what average means."

"Yes, Mr. McPhee. It means . . . "
he began.

But now he knew the whole class

was looking at him. Rick's face started to go red. As red as the lipstick on a Barbie doll. And he forgot what he was going to say.

"What was the word again?" he asked.

Some of the children laughed. Especially Sumo, the biggest boy in

the school, who laughed so much his body shook.

"Can anybody tell Rick what the word is?" said Mr. McPhee.

"Average," said Sumo, poking his tongue out. It was a long tongue, it poked out a long way. Rick could see bits of Sumo's lunch on it.

Rick was confused. "It means average," he said. "Average means average."

And now all the children laughed. Rick's face was even redder. Like a fire engine.

2

WALKING HOME

After school, Rick cut across the football field on his way home.

Football training had started and Mr. McPhee was standing in the center of the field, a football under each arm, barking orders. Ray Goalsneak, a kid in Rick's class, jumped high and had a beautiful catch.

Rick thought about what Mr. McPhee had said earlier. Average. Not good. Not bad. Ray's definitely not average,

thought Rick. Even when his team
loses he still catches a bunch of goals.

Rick started to think about all the
other kids in his class. Susy Cantrill
had a beautiful voice. She'd already
won prizes at singing competitions.
She's definitely not average either,
thought Rick.

Tommy Canadd was amazing at math. Trudy Bigstroke was the best swimmer in the school. They were all good at something. All of them.

Only me, thought Rick. I'm Mr. Average. Not good. Not bad. Mr. Middle-of-the-road.

3

RECIPES

Rick was sitting in the kitchen, his homework spread over the table. Precious the cat jumped from the floor to the chair and from there onto the table. He scowled at Rick, swiping at Rick's pencil with his paw.

"Mom, Precious is annoying me."

"Not now," said Mrs. Bickworth. "I'm busy making a cake."

Mrs. Bickworth was always making cakes.

She baked cakes for the family.
She baked cakes for the neighbors.
She baked cakes for relatives (no
matter how distant). She baked cakes
for birthdays, for marriages, even for
funerals. Every September she baked

a cake for the competition at the County Fair. And every September she came second to Mrs. Havisham.

"OK, Mom," said Rick.

Mrs. Bickworth smiled. What a perfect child I have, she thought. He never argues. He never answers back. A perfect, perfect child.

"Let's see," she said, her finger on the recipe. "One cup of flour."

Cooking, according to Mrs. Bickworth, was a science. And recipes were devised in laboratories, by scientists in spotless white coats. She had no time for those cooking programs on television with their "touch" of this and their "dash" of that. Nonsense! There was nothing scientific about "touch" and "dash."

Mrs. Bickworth piled flour onto her Gottleib-Schmidt scales. They were special scales, scientific scales, accurate to an ounce. She'd had them imported especially from Germany. They were expensive but worth every cent, she said.

When the needle was exactly on eight ounces, she sifted the flour into the bowl, a fine white cloud rising in the air.

She returned to the recipe. Two eggs, it said. Eggs worried Mrs.

Bickworth. Eggs were not scientific. She knew for a fact that her eggs, from her chickens (her happy, well-fed chickens), were much bigger than shop-bought eggs. She'd even written letters to the Egg Board, but as yet she hadn't received a satisfactory explanation.

She cracked the eggs into the bowl and carefully began to mix the ingredients with a wooden spoon.

The phone rang from the other room. Rick answered it.

"Mom, it's Mrs. Nicholson," he said. "She wants to talk about the Fair."

"Bother," said Mrs. Bickworth,

looking down at the bowl.

Once she'd started mixing, she didn't like to stop. The cake never seemed to come out as good as it should.

"Can you keep mixing this for me, Rick?"

Rick hated to be interrupted while he was doing his homework. But his mom had asked, so he'd do it.

"Sure, Mom. I'd love to," he replied.

Mrs. Bickworth smiled. A perfect, perfect child.

Rick looked into the bowl. How many cake mixtures had he seen in his life? Countless. Too many. He

stirred the mixture a couple of times
with the spoon.

"That's funny," he muttered.
"Something's not right."

He held the spoon up and let the
mixture dribble back into the bowl.
Definitely not right. Suddenly a word

appeared in his head. FLOUR. Then another word. MORE. Then another. NEEDS.

FLOUR MORE NEEDS.

Huh, what does that mean? The words rearranged themselves.

MORE NEEDS FLOUR.

Still didn't make sense. Again the words rearranged themselves.

NEEDS MORE FLOUR.

Of course, thought Rick, the mixture needs more flour! He peeked through the door. His mother was still on the phone.

Rick took a tablespoon and dipped it into the flour. He added the extra

flour to the bowl, stirring it in quickly
so it disappeared into the mixture.

That's better, thought Rick. But...

Another word appeared in his head.
Now there were four of them.

FLOUR MORE NEEDS STILL.

They rearranged themselves.

STILL NEEDS MORE FLOUR.

Again Rick dipped the tablespoon into the flour to add more to the mixture.

"Stop!"

Rick turned around. Mrs. Bickworth was standing there, hands on her hips.

"What's going on here?"

"I just thought the mixture could use a touch more flour," said Rick.

"A touch more flour!"

Mrs. Bickworth was very surprised. Rick was the perfect child, after all. She took the spoon from her son and emptied the flour back into the container.

"The recipe said one cup of flour and that's how much I put in. You can't go fiddling around with recipes, young man. Never know where you'll end up."

"Of course, Mom."

Rick went back to his homework. Just as he'd solved the last algebra problem, the timer on the oven buzzed.

"Look at that," said Rick's mother as she took the cake from the oven, its sweet smell flooding the room. "Perfect! Imagine what would've

happened if you'd added that flour.
There must've been at least two
teaspoons on that spoon. We'd be
looking at a disaster right now.
A terrible, terrible disaster."

4

RICK'S FIRST CAKE

When Rick woke up the next morning, when he put on his clothes, ate his breakfast, went to school, there was something in his head. Something he couldn't ignore. Something that made him do things he didn't really want to do. Like run home after school quicker than he'd ever run home before.

Rick burst through the door, puffing, his face shiny with perspiration.

Mrs. Bickworth was sitting at
the kitchen table reading her favorite
cookbook. *The Scientific Basis of
Cooking* it was called. As she read
she smiled, nodding her head in
agreement.

"Mom!"

Mrs. Bickworth looked up at the

clock. It was only ten past three and it usually took Rick at least twenty minutes to amble home from school.

"Did you get an early start today?" she asked.

"No, Mom," said Rick. "I *have* to bake a cake."

Mrs. Bickworth was surprised. Rick had never shown the least bit of interest in baking cakes.

"No, I don't think that's a good idea. I've just cleaned the kitchen. Besides, we haven't finished that cake from yesterday, and there's a few more in the freezer, just in case."

"No, you don't get it, Mom," said

Rick. "I *have* to bake a cake."

How could he possibly explain it, this thing that had been in his head all day, this thing he couldn't ignore? He noticed the name of the book his mom was reading.

"It's homework, Mom. Science project."

"Science?"

"That's right. Mr. McPhee says cooking is like science."

"Of course it is. Of course it is. Well, if it's a science project . . . what sort of cake?"

"A . . . a . . . a . . . sponge cake. Our science project is to make a sponge cake."

"A sponge cake! That's hardly a suitable cake for a beginner. But if that's what Mr. McPhee suggested."

Mrs. Bickworth took another book from the shelf and flicked the pages until she came to the recipe for Plain Sponge Cake. She propped the book

up on the bench so Rick could see
it clearly.

"As long as you follow this recipe
exactly, you can't go wrong. First,
you'll need—"

"Mom!" Rick interrupted. "I can
do it."

Mrs. Bickworth looked at her son,
surprised. Why, he'd almost snapped
at her!

Rick took the bowl of eggs from
the fridge. He picked up one, weighing
it in his hand. No, not right, not the
egg for me, he thought, putting it
aside. He picked up the next egg. Not
right either.

Mrs. Bickworth looked up from her book. "Rick, what are you doing?"

"Picking out the eggs."

"Unfortunately, there's no such thing as a standard egg. This has long been a particular concern of mine. Use any egg, dear."

"Yes, Mom," said Rick, picking up the next egg.

Fortunately for Rick, the phone rang. It was Mrs. Nicholson again. More discussion about the Fair.

"Got you," he thought, after he'd picked up the fifth egg. It felt right—not too heavy, not too light. It looked right—brown and slightly speckled. It even smelled right. Eventually Rick had four eggs that felt, looked, and smelled right.

He broke them into the bowl. Four googly eyes seemed to stare back at Rick. He weighed out eight ounces of sugar with the Gottleib-Schmidt scales and added it to the bowl. Then he took the beater and kept beating until the mixture was smooth. He weighed out eight ounces of flour and added it to the bowl. Finally, he added a quarter of a pound of butter.

"Beat until the mixture reaches a creamy consistency," said the recipe book.

It was creamy but somehow it didn't look right to Rick. He concentrated on what was inside his head. And he waited. BUTTER was the first word to appear. Then MORE. Then A. Then BIT.

BUTTER MORE A BIT.

Rick didn't even have to wait for the words to rearrange themselves. He took a dollop of butter and flicked it into the mixture.

5

RUINED

The oven timer rang just as Mr. Bickworth arrived home.

"Rick's made a cake," said Mrs. Bickworth.

"Well, that's . . ." started Mr. Bickworth, then he stopped, not quite sure what to say.

Instead he took his newspaper from his back pocket and unrolled it.

"Seems like U2's new album is a welcome return to form for the Irish rockers," he said confidently.

"It looks perfect," said Mrs. Bickworth as she carefully took the cake from the oven.

Rick smiled. His mom was right— it was perfect, the most perfect thing he'd ever seen. And he, Rick Bickworth, had made it.

"Follow the recipe and that's what you get—perfection every time," said Mrs. Bickworth.

"But I didn't," said Rick.

"Didn't what?"

"Follow the silly recipe."

"Of course you did. Four eggs. One cup of sugar . . . "

"No, Mom," said Rick, getting
more and more excited. "I added
more butter."

"But why, Rick?" said Mrs.
Bickworth, bewildered. "Why?"

"It didn't look right, and there's
these words that appear in my head.
They're a bit scrambled but they

make sense if you get them in the right order."

"It's ruined," said Mrs. Bickworth.

"But Mom, look at it. It's not ruined. Like you said, it's perfect."

"Nonsense. It's ruined. What a waste."

"Can't we just taste it?"

"Taste it! You'll poison yourself. Imagine what would happen if scientists didn't follow recipes—there'd be explosions all over the place."

"But Mom . . . "

"Take it up to the chickens. They might eat it."

Rick looked over at his dad for support. "Dad," said Rick. "What do you think?"

Mr. Bickworth looked up from his paper. "Apparently the Hang Seng index dropped by twelve points overnight."

6

Sumo

"What would she know," muttered Rick as he closed the back door and started walking towards the chicken-house, sponge cake in one hand.

"Wicky! Wicky! Wicky!"

Rick looked around. It was Sumo, his next door neighbor, his classmate and his enemy. As usual he was sitting in the tree, wedged between the trunk and a branch, his pudgy legs hanging on either side like sausages.

"Wicky! Wicky! Wicky! Your nose is brown and sticky!"

Ricky knew his nose wasn't brown. He knew it wasn't sticky. But he brought up his hand anyway and felt it.

"Got ya!" said Sumo. He laughed so much the tree shook and the leaves rustled.

"What ya got there anyway, Wicky?"

"Nothing," replied Rick.

"Wicky, Wicky, Wicky. There you go again, telling lies."

Again the tree shook and the leaves rustled.

"So what you got there?"

"It's a cake," said Ricky.

"A cake," repeated Sumo, but the way he said "cake" was very different to the way other people said cake. It

was like a mountaineer talking about Mt. Everest, or a swimmer discussing an Olympic gold medal.

"And what are you doing with that *cake*?"

"I'm giving it to the chickens."

"Cake! Chickens!"

For the biggest boy in the school, Sumo was surprisingly agile. He swung one leg over the branch and slithered down the trunk, his sausage legs gripping hard. He clambered over the fence.

"Let's have a look at this cake," he said, snatching it from Rick's hands.

Turning it around, Sumo inspected

the cake from every angle.

"Hmmm, looks okay."

He sniffed it.

"Hmmm, smells okay."

He looked at Rick suspiciously.

"What's wrong with it then?"

"Nothing. Except I didn't follow the recipe so Mom made me throw it out."

"Why didn't you follow the recipe?" demanded Sumo.

"Because it's not right."

"Not right? Course it's right. It wouldn't be the recipe if it wasn't right."

"You sound just like my mom," said Rick. "Here, give me my cake back."

"Wait a sec," said Sumo. He sniffed the cake again, bringing his nose even closer so the tip pressed against it.

"It does smell good. Shame to waste it on a few chickens."

He brought the cake closer and closer to his mouth. Then he stopped, his eyes narrowing.

"This isn't some sort of trick, is it Wicky?"

"Course not," said Rick.

Sumo took a small bite. He moved the piece of cake from cheek to cheek. He swallowed. And waited. Nothing

happened. The suspicious look disappeared from his face and he opened his mouth wide and crammed the rest of the cake in. When he'd stopped chewing, Rick said, "Well, what did it taste like?"

"Wait," said Sumo. "It takes a while with me."

"But the cake's all gone."

Sumo looked around as if he was about to divulge a terrible secret. He leaned closer.

"You know what a taste bud is, Wicky?"

"Of course I know what a taste bud is."

43

"Do you know where they are."

"In your mouth. On your tongue."

"That's right. In the majority of people the taste buds are in the mouth. But not me, Wicky. I have taste buds in my stomach."

"You mean you can taste food with your stomach?"

"I sure can. And that's why I'm a little . . . you know . . . heavy. When you're a very special person like me, when you have taste buds in your stomach, you want to eat all the time."

"Of course," said Rick, although he wasn't too convinced about taste buds in the stomach. He would ask his dad. Maybe he'd read something about it in the paper.

"OK," said Sumo after a while. "I've received all the information."

"And?"

"That's about the best cake I ever ate. Even better than my mom's. Even better than your mom's."

Rick punched both fists into the air. He felt like Ray Goalsneak when he'd scored his tenth goal, like Sarah Cantrill when she reached a high note.

"I knew it. I knew those words in my head were right," he said, turning

to Sumo again. "But was there anything wrong with it?"

"I just told you it was the best cake I ever ate."

"But there must've been something wrong with it?"

"Well, it was . . . " began Sumo reluctantly.

"Go on," said Rick.

" . . . it was a teensy-weeny bit dry."

"Dry, you say."

"Look, only a teensy-weeny bit."

"But dry."

"Rick!" yelled Mrs. Bickworth through the window. "Dinner's ready!"

"I gotta go," said Rick.

"Look Wicky . . . I mean Ricky," said
Sumo. "If you have any more cakes
you want to give to the chickens then
give me a yell. I'll be more than happy
to get rid of them for you."

Sumo rubbed his stomach. "Not

many people have taste buds where I've got them."

"Sure," said Rick.

That night Rick couldn't sleep. He kept tossing and turning in his bed. A teensy-weeny bit dry, Sumo had said. But why? Too much flour? Too much sugar? Not enough milk? Rick realized there was only one way to find out. He had to make another cake and another cake and another cake. And he had to keep on making cakes until he made a cake that wasn't a teensy-weeny bit dry or a teensy-weeny bit sweet, that wasn't a teensy-weeny bit anything except perfect.

7

PROBLEM

It was lunchtime at Cobdolla
Elementary School and in the corner
of the playground, sitting under the
shade of a tree, were Rick and Sumo.
Occasionally one of the other kids
would stop and stare at the two of
them. Sumo and Rick had been
enemies since kindergarten. It was
like seeing a mouse snuggling up to
a cat. The other kids would've been
even more amazed if they heard

what Rick and Sumo were talking
about. Because Rick and Sumo were
talking about cakes. Especially the
cake Rick was going to make as soon
as he got home that night.

"Why don't you make a banana

cake? I love banana cakes," said Sumo.

"Because I need to get that sponge cake right first," answered Rick.

Suddenly their conversation was interrupted by a booming voice over the loudspeaker. "Would Rick Bickworth and Sam Gourman please report to Mr. McPhee's office immediately."

"Don't tell him anything," said Sumo as they walked across the playground.

Rick had only been to Mr. McPhee's office a couple of times. It was just like he remembered it—posters of football players on the walls and dusty football trophies inside a glass cabinet. As for Sumo, he seemed right at home.

"That's new, isn't it?" he asked, pointing to a glossy poster of a famous quarterback.

Mr. McPhee, sitting behind his desk, ignored the question.

"What's going on with you two?" he demanded.

Rick looked at Sumo. Sumo looked at Rick.

"Nothing," they replied simultaneously.

"Nonsense," said Mr. McPhee. "I've been a teacher for twenty-seven years. I know when something's going on."

"I can assure you, Mr. McPhee, it's nothing," said Sumo smoothly.

Mr. McPhee turned his attention to Rick, fixing him with his laser stare.

Sumo nudged Rick with his elbow. Tell him nothing!

"Well?" said Mr. McPhee.

Rick could feel himself wilting under the intensity of Mr. McPhee's gaze. It was too much for Rick—he didn't have Sumo's office experience. He blurted out the whole story.

When he'd finished, Mr. McPhee looked up at the wall, his eyes resting on the champion quarterback.

"Our football team's getting beaten by five goals every game, and you two, the biggest boys in the school, are worried about cakes!"

Rick sunk down in his chair.

"Cakes!" repeated McPhee in disgust.

Rick sunk down even further.

"There's nothing wrong with eating cakes," said Sumo.

Rick looked at Sumo. He was sitting up in his chair, looking straight at Mr. McPhee, straight into his terrible laser stare.

"Nothing wrong at all."

Well, thought Rick, if Sumo can do it, I can too. He sat up. Squared his shoulders. Took a deep breath.

"Nothing wrong with making cakes either."

Mr. McPhee looked at him, surprised.

"In fact, I love making cakes,"

continued Rick. "It's the only time I haven't felt average. Middle-of-the-road. Mediocre."

"There's nothing average about Rick's cakes," said Sumo. "You should taste them, Mr. McPhee!"

Again Mr. McPhee looked up at the champion quarterback for inspiration.

"I don't like problems in my school," he said finally. "I want to see you both after class."

For the rest of the afternoon Rick couldn't concentrate on his work. What was going to happen to him? What punishment did Mr. McPhee have in mind?

For the second time that day Rick
and Sumo sat in Mr. McPhee's office.

"It's all arranged," said Mr. McPhee.

What is arranged? thought Rick in
a panic.

Mr. McPhee continued. "Mrs.
Singh, the home economics teacher at

the high school, is expecting you on Tuesday afternoons between 3:15 and 4:30. She said you can even use their ingredients if you like."

Rick could hardly believe what he'd heard. "Thanks," he said. "Thanks a lot."

Mr. McPhee looked at his watch. "Well, I must go. Training starts in ten minutes and we're playing away on Saturday."

The two boys walked home together, talking about cakes. Sumo kept rubbing his stomach. "I can almost taste them," he kept saying. "Almost taste them."

Rick's mom was in a great mood when he arrived home and the rest was easy. Much easier than Rick had expected.

"Sumo and I are doing a project after school on Tuesdays so I'll be late home on that day," he said quickly, getting it all out in one breath.

"That's wonderful, Rick. Besides, it'll get you out of my way. The Fair's coming up and I've got plenty of baking to do."

"Mom, it's ten weeks away."

"You can never get too much practice," she said.

"You said you would never enter

again. You said you were sick of coming second to Mrs. Havisham."

Mrs. Bickworth smiled. "A little birdy told me something today. Something very interesting."

8

RICK AND SUMO AT
THE HIGH SCHOOL

Every Tuesday after school, Rick and
Sumo walked over to the high school.
Every Tuesday Rick baked a cake.
Every Tuesday Sumo ate that cake.

"Well?" Rick would ask impatiently.

"Wait," Sumo would reply. "It takes
time with me. You see I've got . . ."

"I know. I know. Taste buds in your
stomach."

"Without a doubt the best cake I've

ever eaten," Sumo would eventually reply, licking his lips to make sure he had captured every last crumb.

"But there must be something wrong with it," Rick would say.

"I told you, it's the best cake I've ever eaten."

"But there must be *something* wrong."

"OK, if you insist. It's a teensy-weeny bit dry," Sumo would say. Or a teensy-weeny bit sweet. Or a teensy-weeny bit heavy.

But on this Tuesday, the last Tuesday before the school break began, something was wrong.

"Oh my guts!" groaned Sumo, clutching at his stomach. "Oh, my aching guts!"

No, that can't be possible, thought Rick. Sumo's guts are made of cast-iron. They're coated with Teflon. They're bulletproof and nuclear resistant. But now, when he really needed Sumo's guts and their extraordinary taste buds, they weren't available.

"C'mon, Sumo," said Rick, "I'm sure this is the best cake yet."

Sumo looked at the cake cooling on the rack. It certainly looked like the best cake yet. He sniffed the air. It certainly smelled like the best cake yet. Sumo had no doubt it would taste like the best cake yet. Each week Rick's cakes had got better and better.

But Sumo had a plan. "Oh, my aching guts!" he groaned, clutching again at his stomach.

Well, somebody has to taste it,
thought Rick as he took a knife. But
before he could cut a slice, Sumo
grabbed his wrist. Again Rick was
surprised by how quickly Sumo
could move.

"No. Don't ruin it!" yelled Sumo.

"I'll take it home. Try it tonight."

Sumo's acting pretty weird, thought Rick, but taking the cake home was the best solution. After all, only Sumo had taste buds in his stomach.

"How was it?" Rick asked Sumo the next day at school.

"How was what?"

"The cake of course."

"Oh, the cake. It was . . . um . . . it was . . . very special."

"Special?" asked Rick, but Sumo had already started walking away.

9

THE SHOW

The County Fair was the biggest day of the year in Cobdolla. People came from all over the area. From Lyrup. From Qualco. From Overland Corner. They even came from as far as Katmandook.

Rick and his parents went to all the events. But Mrs. Bickworth couldn't stop fidgeting in her seat, couldn't stop looking at her watch.

"Mom, what's wrong?" said Rick finally.

"Remember that little birdy?"
replied Mrs. Bickworth.

"The one that Precious brought in?
Without its head?"

"No, silly. The little birdy who told
me the little secret about the Fair."

Rick nodded.

"Well, the little birdy was right. Mrs. Havisham didn't enter this year. She thought it was time to give somebody else a chance."

Sumo walked past, pink cotton candy in one hand and a corn dog in the other.

"Hi, Rick," he said. "You'd better be going to the awards."

"We're all going," butted in Mrs. Bickworth. "It's going to be a very special night."

"It sure is," said Sumo, winking at Rick.

Rick, not knowing what else to do, winked back.

"He's a peculiar boy," said Mrs. Bickworth after Sumo had left. "Always has been."

Mr. Bickworth looked up from his paper. "Appears that BHP has posted a record first-quarter profit this year."

10

THE AWARDS

The hall was packed. Wow, just about everybody in Cobdolla must be here, thought Rick. As well as all those people from Lyrup, Qualco, Overland Corner, and Katmandook.

Mrs. Bickworth insisted they push their way to the front. "It'll be much easier to get up on the stage from here," she said.

The judges for the various categories were seated on the stage. Next to them,

on a felt-covered table, were the winning ribbons—green for third, red for second, and blue for first.

First award was for the Fancy Bantam. The next award, for Sow with Litter, was won by Mrs. Parson. Rick clapped loudly. He liked pigs and he'd especially liked Mrs. Parson's huge pig with her cute babies. The awards kept on coming—Finest Wool, Prize Bull, Best Marmalade—until there was only one award left: Cake of the Fair. Mrs. Bickworth took a little mirror from her handbag and checked her makeup. She wanted to look her best in front of all these people.

Mrs. Myerson, head of the cake judging panel, mentioned that the winner would go on to the State final contest. Then she talked about the very high standard of entries. How, despite this, the winning cake really did stand out. How, in terms of appearance, taste and texture, it was not only clearly the best cake this year, but one of the best cakes she'd ever judged.

As Mrs. Myerson talked, Mrs. Bickworth became more and more embarrassed, her face redder and redder.

"The winner of Cake of the Fair is . . . " Mrs. Myerson paused dramatically.

Mrs. Bickworth straightened her dress, patted her hair and took a step towards the stage.

" . . . Rick Bickworth!" said Mrs. Myerson.

Mrs. Bickworth kept walking towards the stage.

"I repeat, *Rick* Bickworth," said Mrs. Myerson.

Mrs. Bickworth froze.

"But . . . but . . . but I didn't enter a cake," said Rick.

"But I did," came a voice from behind. Sumo's voice.

"Is Rick out there somewhere?" asked Mrs. Myerson.

"He's right here!" yelled Sumo, taking Rick by the elbow and steering him towards the stage.

As he received the blue ribbon from Mrs. Myerson, Rick looked out into the crowd. He could see them all out there. And they were all clapping. Sally Quickfire. Nathan Longdob. Laura Cantrill. Even Mr. McPhee. They were all clapping because he, Rick Bickworth, had made a cake that wasn't average, that wasn't middle-of-

the-road, that wasn't mediocre. He'd made the best cake of the whole Fair.

"This is a real family affair," said Mrs. Myerson. "Because the red ribbon for runner-up goes to Rick's mother, Mrs. Bickworth."

In all the excitement, Rick had forgotten about his mother, but now he could see her standing at the front of the crowd, staring at Rick's blue ribbon in disbelief.

"Mrs. Bickworth?" prompted Mrs. Myerson, waving the red ribbon.

Rick had never seen his mom run before. In fact, he thought she'd lost the ability years ago. But by the time

she reached the exit door, by the time
all those people from Cobdolla, Lyrup,
Overland Corner, and even
Katmandook parted to let her
through, Mrs. Bickworth was
definitely running. Not only that, she
was crying as well. The wooden floor
behind her was sprinkled with tears.

11

THE FEUD

Sunday dinner at the Bickworths was always a big deal: roast chicken, roast potatoes, roast pumpkin, and all the trimmings. After Rick had cleared away the dishes, Mrs. Bickworth put a cake on the table.

Mr. Bickworth looked suspiciously at the cake, inspecting it from all angles. Mr. Bickworth took a spoonful of the cake and put it into his mouth. He moved that spoonful from cheek to

cheek. And he spat it out. Right onto the tablecloth.

Mr. Bickworth spoke. For once, it wasn't something that he'd read in the paper. There was no mention of U2, the Hang-Seng, or BHP's record first-quarter profit.

"Not fit for pigs," he said. "Where

did this come from?"

"The supermarket," replied Mrs. Bickworth.

"The supermarket?" said Mr. Bickworth, getting the words out quickly like he couldn't even stand their putrid taste in his mouth.

He glared at Rick. Rick knew exactly what the glare meant. This, young man, is entirely your fault.

Since the Fair, since she'd been awarded the red ribbon for the second-best cake and sprinkled the wooden floor of the hall with her tears, Mrs. Bickworth had stopped baking. Of course, Rick had explained it all to his mom. How it wasn't his fault that his cake had won the blue ribbon. How he hadn't entered the competition, Sumo had. But it was no good—Mrs. Bickworth had packed away the Gottleib-Schmidt scales and put all her recipe books into a cupboard.

"I'd like some proper cake," said Mr. Bickworth, looking at his wife.

But Mrs. Bickworth just shook her head.

"Please, dear," he said.

"Please, Mom," said Rick.

Again she shook her head.

Rick wished he'd never baked that stupid cake, never won that blue ribbon. Now his father glared at him all the time and his mother hardly talked to him. It was better when he was average. When he was middle-of-the-road. When he was mediocre.

When the phone rang, Rick immediately said, "I'll get it!" It was a

good excuse to get out of the kitchen.

It was Mrs. Myerson. She wanted to talk about the State final.

"What if I don't enter a cake?" asked Rick.

"But you must," said Mrs. Myerson. "With your talent you have a good chance to win."

"But what if I don't enter?" said Rick, impatiently.

"Well, I'd have to consult the rule book, but I'm pretty sure the runner-up would then get the opportunity."

Perfect, thought Rick.

"In that case, I resign," he said, and he put down the phone.

12

BORN TO BAKE

"Eight ounces of flour," said Mrs. Bickworth to herself, reading from *The Scientific Basis of Cooking*.

Rick looked up from his homework and smiled. It had all gone according to plan.

Mrs. Bickworth weighed out the flour exactly, using the Gottleib-Schmidt scales.

Then she weighed out the sugar exactly.

So it went. Mrs. Bickworth
measuring out the ingredients exactly,
until the mixture was ready.

Mrs. Bickworth closed the recipe
book and sighed.

"What do you think?" she asked
her son.

"I think the ingredients were weighed accurately and I think it's going to be a very scientific cake," he replied.

"No. I mean what do you really think?"

"What do I really, really think?"

"Yes, what do you really, really think?"

Rick stood up and looked at the mixture. Suddenly a word popped into his head. Then another one. And another.

MORE NEEDS A FLOUR BIT.

"I think it needs a bit more flour," he said tentatively.

"A bit more?" repeated Mrs. Bickworth suspiciously.

"Let's see," said Rick. "I think it needs one teaspoon."

"That's better. That's more scientific," said Mrs. Bickworth, weighing out that exact amount of flour in ounces and adding it to the mixture. "Is that all?"

"A touch . . . I mean, exactly seven hundredths of an ounce of sugar," said Rick.

Mrs. Bickworth measured out seven hundredths of an ounce of sugar and added it to the bowl.

"It looks fine now, Mom."

"This is just a test," said Mrs. Bickworth as she poured the mixture into the cake tin. "But if it turns out okay, we can make the real one tomorrow."

"We?" asked Rick.

"Yes, you and me."

"But I resigned," said Rick.

"Nonsense," said Mrs. Bickworth.

The oven timer rang just as Mr. Bickworth arrived home.

"Is that cake I smell?" said Mr. Bickworth, excitedly.

There was a knock on the door. It was Sumo.

"I smelled something," was all he said.

As Mrs. Bickworth took the cake from the oven, Rick put out four plates.

"Well?" said Mrs. Bickworth after they'd all finished.

"Still getting information," said Sumo.

"Sumo's got taste buds in his stomach," Rick told his parents.

"I think I might've read something about that in the paper," said Mr. Bickworth, helping himself to a second serving.

"It is, without doubt, the best cake I have ever tasted," said Sumo.

He looked at Mrs. Bickworth.

"Even better than the one that won the award."

Mrs. Bickworth smiled at Rick.

"You were born to bake," she said. "Born to bake."